Double Trouble Monsters

by **Marcia Thornton Jones**
and
Debbie Dadey

illustrated by **John Steven Gurney**

A
LITTLE APPLE
PAPERBACK

SCHOLASTIC INC.
New York   Toronto   London   Auckland   Sydney
Mexico City   New Delhi   Hong Kong

5969126

*To John Steven Gurney and all his
monstrously wonderful art! — MTJ*

*For Doug, Sharon, Elizabeth, and
Christine Wathen — DD*

ISBN 0-439-05870-8

Text copyright © 1999 by Marcia Thornton Jones and Debra S. Dadey.
Illustrations copyright © 1999 by Scholastic Inc.
All rights reserved. Published by Scholastic Inc.
LITTLE APPLE PAPERBACKS is a trademark of Scholastic Inc.
THE ADVENTURES OF THE BAILEY SCHOOLS KIDS in design is
a registered trademark of Scholastic Inc.

12 11 10 9 8 7 6 5 4 3 2   9/9 0 1/0 2/0 3/0 4/0

Printed in the U.S.A.   40

First Scholastic printing, March 1999

Contents

1

Tree House

Ben stopped pounding nails and dropped the hammer near Annie's sneakers.

"Watch it," she warned, "or I'll hammer your head."

"I am watching," Ben whispered. "I just don't believe what I see."

Ben and his little sister, Annie, were putting the finishing touches on a super-duper tree house between their house and Hauntly Manor Inn.

"It's only Jane," Annie told her brother. Jane was their neighbor and Annie's best friend. "She said she'd help us."

Jane scrambled up to where Ben and Annie were perched. From their tree house in the old maple tree the kids were able to see all the way down Dedman Street.

"I'm not worried about Jane," Ben said.

1

"I'm worried about what just turned down Dedman Street."

Jane and Annie looked where Ben pointed. A long black station wagon slowly drove down the street and stopped in front of their next-door neighbors' house. A car in front of Hauntly Manor wasn't unusual. After all, the huge house next to them was a bed-and-breakfast. It even had a big sign hanging in the front yard. But this was no normal car.

"There is only one kind of car that is long and black and has curtains hanging in the back windows," Ben said. "A hearse."

A chilly breeze ruffled the new leaves on the maple tree, and Jane shivered. "What would a hearse be doing at Hauntly Manor Inn?" she asked.

The house at 13 Dedman Street was brand-new when the Hauntlys moved next door to Ben and Annie. Now the black shutters hung at crazy angles and paint peeled in long, curling strips. Several porch railings were broken and jagged cracks were etched in all the windows. Even the trees and grass had died. Annie and Ben were sure their new neighbors were monsters and that Hauntly Manor Inn was a monster hotel.

"There's only one kind of guest that would drive a car like that," Ben said quietly. "A monster guest."

2

Secret

"The Hauntlys' new guest is definitely not the life of the party!" Ben joked.

"Very funny, coffin breath," Annie said.

The door to the hearse slowly swung open. The kids heard it squeak from their hiding place in the tree. A man with gray hair stepped out of the car. He wore thick black glasses and was so short his head barely reached the top of the car.

"He is definitely having a bad hair day," Ben said with a laugh. It was true. The stranger's hair looked as though he'd been caught in a windstorm going three hundred miles an hour.

"That's not very nice," Annie said.

"Yeah, maybe he can't help the way he looks," Jane said.

"Just like you can't help the way you stink," Ben said.

Jane curled her fingers in a fist and held it below Ben's nose. "You won't be smelling anything for weeks unless you take that back."

"Shhh," Annie warned. "The Hauntlys are coming outside."

The three kids ducked down and peered over the top of the tree house walls as the heavy wooden door to Hauntly Manor Inn slowly swung open. Suddenly, a wild tangle of fur dashed through the door and headed straight for the maple tree.

"Watch out!" Ben warned. "Kilmer's cat just escaped."

The girls dodged a blur of claws as the cat scrambled up the tree. The kids knew all about Kilmer's cat. Sparky was black and tore around the inn as if she had just eaten jalapeño-flavored jumping beans. The kids never petted Sparky. They didn't dare.

"That was a close call," Annie said,

brushing a clump of fur from her sweat-shirt.

"Forget about Sparky," Jane said. "Look what the Hauntlys are doing."

Boris Hauntly's black cape was so long it covered his feet. He looked like he floated down the sidewalk. The sun glinted off the huge red button at Boris' throat. Jane thought it looked exactly like a giant drop of blood.

Hilda hurried after her husband, Boris. Her wild hair stuck up in crazy directions, and her long white lab coat was spotted with new stains.

Hilda and Boris went straight to the back of the hearse and swung the rear door open. Hilda looked up and down the side-walk while Boris and the stranger reached inside, pulling out a long skinny crate.

"What could be in that?" Annie asked.

"Whatever it is," Ben said, "Hilda acts like she doesn't want anyone to see."

"I don't like the looks of this," Jane said.

"A secret box hidden in the back of a hearse can only mean trouble."

Just then the tree house shook, branches swayed, and leaves trembled.

"Hang on for your lives!" Ben shrieked. "It's an earthquake!"

Jane grabbed a limb. "No," she said. "It's only Kilmer."

Kilmer Hauntly popped his head through the opening in the floor of the tree house and grinned at his three friends. Kilmer was in the same fourth-grade class as Ben and Jane, but he didn't look like a normal fourth-grader. He was at least a foot taller than Ben and his hair was cut straight across the top. He looked exactly like a young Frankenstein's monster.

"I have been looking for you," Kilmer said. "I have wonderful news. My father has invited you to meet our newest guest."

"How nice," Annie said in her most polite voice.

"We can come right now," Ben said.

"NO!" Kilmer yelled. "My mother and our guest have important work to do. Come tomorrow at eight o'clock." Then Kilmer slid down the tree and hurried back to Hauntly Manor Inn.

"That was strange," Jane said. "Kilmer usually sticks around to play."

"Maybe he wanted to talk to their new guest," Ben said.

"That can't be," Annie said. "Hilda and the stranger have to work."

"What kind of visitor would work with Hilda?" Ben asked.

"I know," Jane said slowly. "A mad scientist!"

3

The Professor

"Are you sure it's safe?" Annie asked.

It was the next day and Ben, Jane, and Annie walked up the sidewalk in front of Hauntly Manor Inn. Ben was jumping on every crack they passed; there were lots of cracks with long weeds sticking up from them.

"Look," Annie said. A tree's dead branches reached down toward the kids like long bony skeleton fingers, but that's not what Annie noticed. She was pointing to two huge owls perched in the top branches. Their heads slowly turned so they could keep their eyes on the kids as they passed beneath their perch.

Jane took a deep breath. "As long as we stick together, we won't have to worry."

"I'm already worried," Ben said. "But not about owls or mad scientists. I'm worried because I'm stuck with two mad girls."

"Ben," Annie said. "We don't know that the Hauntlys' visitor is a mad scientist."

The kids climbed the stairs leading to the front porch at Hauntly Manor Inn. When they reached the top step, two identical lizards scurried across the porch and disappeared over the edge into the dead branches of a bush.

"If the strange visitor is a scientist, and he's visiting the Hauntlys, then we need to be careful," Jane pointed out. "Very careful."

"I'll be careful," Ben said as he lifted the heavy doorknocker and then let it fall. "I'll be careful to stay away from the crazy girls on Dedman Street!"

The wooden door slowly creaked open and the three kids came face-to-face with their friend. Kilmer smiled and opened the door wider. "Please," he said, "do come in. We have been waiting for you."

The three kids followed Kilmer into the dark living room of Hauntly Manor Inn. No one was in the room, so Jane, Annie, and Ben perched on the edge of the red velvet sofa. Annie stuck her legs straight out in front of her. She was sure she saw the giant claw feet of the sofa moving when they came into the room.

Boris pushed through a swinging door and smiled down at the three kids. Jane couldn't help noticing his pointy eyeteeth. If it weren't for his bright orange hair, Boris could be Dracula's twin brother. Boris set a steaming tray of slimy noodles on a table in front of the kids. Ben decided they looked liked vulture intestines.

"I have prepared special treats today," Boris said in his Transylvanian accent, "in honor of our special guest."

Just then Hilda came through the swinging door. Following her was the Hauntlys' guest. He wasn't much taller than Kilmer and his gray hair still stuck straight up in

the air. He set another tray down next to the first tray. Ben was hoping for cookies, and he was disappointed to see that the stranger's tray carried the same wiggly noodles as Boris' tray.

"This," Hilda said with a smile, "is my associate, Professor E. Gore!"

Professor E. Gore smiled at the kids. "The pleasure is mine," he said as he shook each of their hands. "Kilmer has told me all about you." It sounded like all the letters got stuck on Professor E. Gore's tongue when he spoke.

"Are you from Transylvania?" Annie asked.

Professor E. Gore shook his head. "*Nein* . . . er . . . I mean *no*," Professor E. Gore said. "Please, try our treats. I helped Boris whip these up just for you."

Ben's stomach rumbled, but he shook his head. "I'm trying to lose weight," he said. "I'll let Annie and Jane have my share."

Annie gulped. "I just ate before I came. Jane can have all mine."

Jane shook her head. "I'm allergic to . . . um . . . noodly things."

"What a shame," Boris said. "Perhaps I could find something else in the kitchen."

"NO," Jane blurted. "I mean, thanks, but I'm really not hungry."

"Well," Professor E. Gore said. "I am glad to finally meet Kilmer's friends. But I am afraid I have work to do."

"Yes," Hilda said. "We are so close to the answer."

Hilda and Professor E. Gore hurried from the room while Boris carried one of the trays back to the kitchen. Kilmer followed with the other tray.

"Did you see his lab coat?" Jane whispered as soon as they were alone in the room. "It's just like the one Hilda wears."

Hilda Hauntly was a scientist at F.A.T.S., the Federal Aeronautics Technology Station. She always wore a long white coat that was covered in purple and green stains. The kids were sure she cooked up strange concoctions in her private laboratory at Hauntly Manor.

"Professor E. Gore's coat has the same stains on it as Hilda's," Annie noticed. "Jane was right. Professor E. Gore must be a scientist."

"Why would a scientist be visiting Hauntly Manor?" Jane asked.

Just then a black cloud of fur streaked through the living room. It stopped long enough to look at the three kids on the couch and hiss. Ben, Annie, and Jane lifted their feet off the floor, away from Sparky. The cat hissed once more and darted through the swinging door.

"Whew," Ben said. "That was close."

But then another whirlwind of fur skidded into the living room. The second cat blinked its yellow eyes at the kids before digging its claws into the floor and taking off after the first cat.

"Oh, no," Jane said. "The Hauntlys got another cat and it's exactly like Sparky."

"It's much worse than that," Annie said. "If I'm right, we may be in trouble. Double trouble!"

4
Double Everything

"Let's get out of here," Annie squealed. The three kids rushed out of Hauntly Manor Inn and up into their tree house.

"It wasn't very nice not to say good-bye to the Hauntlys," Jane told Annie.

"What's wrong with you, anyway?" Ben asked Annie. "Why did you have to rush off? I wanted to ask Kilmer to play base-ball."

Annie leaned back into the shadows of the tree house. It was starting to get dark and many of the houses below them were turning on their lights. "I have to tell you something about Professor E. Gore," Annie said. "I think he's a mad scientist who's come here to teach Hilda how to make dou-bles of everything."

Ben looked at Jane. They both burst out

21

laughing. "Are you nuts?" Ben asked Annie. "Professor E. Gore is just a regular guest, taking a vacation at the Hauntlys'."

"Well, there were two trays of food," Annie said slowly. "And there were two of Kilmer's cats."

"And don't forget the twin owls and lizards," Jane reminded them.

Ben rolled his eyes. "And two crazy girls in one tree house."

Annie gulped. "What if it's true?" she asked.

Ben smiled. "I think it would be cool. Just think. We could have double of everything — double chocolate bars, double milk shakes, and double computer games."

"And double teachers," Annie said, pointing out the tree house to the sidewalk. The kids saw one of the third-grade teachers marching up the street toward the Hauntlys'. Mrs. Jeepers wore a bright purple dress with green polka dots. A big green brooch was pinned on her collar. She was so strange some kids thought she was a vampire. Annie was glad she was in another third-grade class.

"What if Hilda doubled Mrs. Jeepers?" Annie said. "Two vampire teachers would be the end of Bailey City."

"If Hilda doubled all the teachers, it would mean double homework!" Jane said.

"There are already too many teachers in Bailey City, if you ask me," Ben said, "and there's definitely too much homework."

Jane gulped. "This is serious!"

Ben held up his hand. "Wait just a minute. You guys are jumping the gun. First of all, Professor E. Gore is just a regular guy. Second of all, they aren't doubling anything."

Jane watched as Mrs. Jeepers went inside Hauntly Manor. "I guess there's only one thing left for us to do," Jane said. "We have to prove it."

"And I know exactly how we can do it," Annie said.

"How?" Jane and Ben asked together.

"Look." Annie pointed to a room in

Hauntly Manor. The light had just come on and the kids could see clearly into the room through the window.

"It's Hilda's laboratory," Ben said. They knew Hilda had a laboratory at home and by all the test tubes they saw through the window, they could tell that must be it. Mrs. Jeepers, Hilda, and Professor E. Gore entered the laboratory and went straight over to two large wooden tables. Two long figures, covered by white sheets, lay on the tables.

"Those lumps look like they have feet," Annie said nervously.

"They look like people," Ben said matter-of-factly.

"If they're people," Jane whispered, "they don't look alive."

"Oh, no," Jane gasped. "The Hauntlys are making monsters. We *are* in trouble! Double MONSTER trouble!"

5

Two Bens

"What's the big deal?" Ben asked. "I think it would be cool to have a double. Then I wouldn't have to do a thing. My double could go to school for me. He could do my homework for me. I'd make him eat my spinach for me and do my chores. It would be fantastic!"

Annie rolled her eyes. "I don't think the world could stand two Bens."

"Shhh," Jane hissed. "We're not the only ones spying on the Hauntlys."

"What are you talking about?" Annie asked.

Jane pointed to the bushes outside the laboratory window. "Someone's hiding in there." Sure enough, the kids saw the bushes moving.

"You know what this means, don't you?" Jane asked.

Ben nodded. "The Hauntlys are popular."

"No," Jane said. "It means whoever is there is close enough to hear."

"That means they'll know how to make doubles of everything, too," Annie whispered.

"Exactly," Jane said. "And if whoever is listening is bad, the whole world may be in big trouble!"

Ben smiled. "Lucky for you guys I made this tree house with a super-duper escape plan. I can catch whoever is listening. Watch this." Ben reached into the dark tree limbs and pulled out a long heavy rope.

"That looks dangerous," Jane pointed out.

"I'll be just like an ape man," Ben grunted. "I'm king of the jungle."

"You're a nut," Jane grunted back.

"You'd better be careful," Annie warned Ben.

Ben held on to the rope and got ready to jump off the tree house. "I'm always careful." Without another word he closed his eyes and swung on the rope. Ben swung in the direction of the Hauntlys' laboratory.

Unfortunately, he didn't swing far enough. He swung right into the Hauntlys' garbage cans.

Clang! Clang! Garbage flew everywhere. Annie thought she heard Sparky yowl. Whoever was in the bushes scrambled away.

"We'd better check on Ben," Annie said. "I hope he didn't hurt himself." The two girls hurried down the tree house ladder and over to Ben. They found him sitting on a pile of trash with an old banana peel on his head.

Jane laughed. "You look more like a monkey than the king of the jungle."

Ben threw the banana peel at Jane and got up out of the garbage.

"Are you sure you're okay?" Annie asked, helping put the garbage back in the cans.

"I'm fine," Ben grumbled. "Just a little stinky."

"That's nothing new," Jane giggled.

"The bad thing is that whoever was listening ran off," Annie said. "Now we may never know who the spy is or what the Hauntlys are planning."

Jane threw a can into the recycling bin and shrugged. "I guess there's nothing we can do about it. I just hope whoever was listening doesn't start doubling things, too!"

6

Dirty Underwear

"I wish we knew for sure what Hilda and Professor E. Gore are up to," Annie said as the three kids walked back to the tree house.

"We could ask Kilmer," Ben suggested.

Annie shook her head. "He didn't seem to want to tell us anything about Professor E. Gore. It was like Kilmer was keeping a secret from us."

"That's not like Kilmer," Ben said.

Jane shrugged. "Maybe Kilmer had to keep this a secret because it's so horrible."

"No," Annie said. "No secret is that bad. You can always tell a friend."

"Well, whatever the secret is, whoever or whatever was listening outside the window knows all about it," Jane said.

Ben leaned against the tree house ladder

and pointed a finger at Jane. "For all you know, Professor E. Gore was just sharing a recipe for chicken soup with Hilda."

"Or maybe he was sharing a recipe for disaster," Jane told him. "Maybe Professor E. Gore has a secret formula for cloning everything from cats to dirty underwear."

Annie giggled. "Ben doesn't need any help in the dirty underwear department. He has them thrown all over his bedroom."

"I do not!" Ben yelled.

"Ben! Annie! It's time to come inside," their mother called out the back door. "Jane, you'd better run on home, too. It's dinnertime."

"Coming," Annie told her mother.

"What are we going to do about Professor E. Gore?" Jane asked.

Annie swatted at a mosquito and scratched her arm. "I guess there's nothing we can do."

"I told you we should just ask Kilmer," Ben said.

Jane smiled and snapped her fingers. "I'll make you a deal. You guys go with me tonight, and tomorrow we'll ask Kilmer whatever you want."

"We can't go anywhere right now," Annie explained. "We have to go inside."

Jane nodded. "We'll sneak out after dark and meet at the tree house. We'll use Kilmer's secret key to sneak inside Hauntly Manor. Then we can see exactly what's lying on those tables in the laboratory."

Annie gulped. "I don't think that's such a good idea. It sounds dangerous."

"Of course it's dangerous," Jane said.

Ben grinned. "That's why I like it."

Jane swatted at a mosquito and checked her watch. "We'll meet back here at exactly ten-thirty."

"But that's past my bedtime," Annie whined.

Jane frowned at Annie. "Do you think evil scientists worry about bedtimes? Do you think bad guys worry about bed-times?"

Ben flexed his muscles. "Do you think super spies worry about bedtimes?"

Annie sighed. "All right. But I have a feeling something horrible is going to happen."

7
Super Sneaks

When the house was totally silent, Ben tiptoed down the hall to his sister's room. Annie was sitting up in bed, waiting for him. "Do you have your flashlight?" Ben whispered.

Annie nodded. "I'm ready if you are."

Ben and Annie sneaked down the hall in their stocking feet. They crept through the kitchen and out the back door, making sure the door didn't make any noise when they closed it.

"Are you sure this is a good idea?" Annie asked as they sat on the back steps and slipped into their sneakers.

"It's a terrible idea," Ben said. "But Jane is right; it's the only way we can find out what the Hauntlys are planning."

Ben and Annie switched on their flashlights and found their way to the bottom of the giant maple tree to wait for Jane. An owl hooted and wings fluttered in the branches over their heads. Somewhere in the distance a dog howled. "I wish Jane would hurry," Annie said. "Nighttime gives me the creeps."

"There's nothing out here that's any different than in the daytime," Ben pointed out. "You just can't see them."

"Exactly," Annie said. "It's what I can't see that worries me."

"Shhh," Ben warned. "I hear something."

Ben and Annie huddled together, listening to the night noises. Sure enough, there was a rustling sound in the bushes near the Hauntlys' backyard. "Oh, no," Annie whimpered. "It's going to get us."

"What?" Ben hissed.

"IT!" Annie told him.

"BOO!" Something jumped out of the bushes, right at Ben and Annie.

"AAAAHHHH!" Ben screamed.

Two hands clapped over his mouth and

cut Ben's scream short. "Are you crazy?" Jane asked, pulling her hands away. "Do you want everybody in Bailey City to hear us?"

"You scared us half to death," Annie told her best friend. "You shouldn't sneak up on people like that."

"Especially in the dead of night," Ben told Jane.

"I was just practicing," Jane said with a grin. "If we're going to find out what's happening in Hilda Hauntly's laboratory, we're going to have to be super sneaks. I just proved that I could do it. Can you?"

Ben stood up straight and puffed out his chest. "If anyone is a super sneak, it's me," he said.

Annie nodded. "I'm ready, too. Let's do it."

The three friends stayed in the darkest shadows and quietly moved toward the Hauntlys' back door. Ben picked up a pot of dead flowers, and Jane reached under it where they knew Kilmer kept a key hidden. Suddenly, Jane gasped.

"What's the matter?" Annie asked.

"I don't think this is what we're looking for," Jane said through clenched teeth. She held up a long wiggly worm.

"Yuck," Annie said. "Maybe we should use our flashlights."

Annie shined her light under the pot on a wriggling mound of worms. Jane shoved them aside and grabbed a copper key. Ben gently put down the pot so he wouldn't squish any of Kilmer's worms.

"Are you ready?" Jane asked.

Ben and Annie nodded. "Ready," they said together.

Jane slipped the key into the keyhole. The door slowly swung open. It was pitch-black inside the Hauntlys' kitchen. Ben shined the tiny beam from his flashlight across the floor. Something skittered under a table to get out of the light.

"Come on," Jane said, pushing open the swinging door that led to the living room. Ben and Annie followed.

The first thing Annie saw was the couch

with the giant claw feet. "I think they moved," Annie whimpered.

"It's just furniture," Ben whispered. "It can't move."

"Then what's that sound?" Annie asked.

The kids stood still. Sure enough, they heard a *click-click-click* like the sound of toenails hitting the floor.

"It can't be," Jane said. "But just to be sure, keep as far away as possible."

They flattened their backs against the wall and made their way across the room. Suddenly, Ben stopped.

"We don't have all night," Jane told him. "Keep moving."

"I can't," Ben said with a gulp. "Something just grabbed my shirt!"

8

Caught!

Annie clicked on her flashlight and shined it right into the eyes of the ugliest creature she'd ever seen. "Run!" she started to scream, but Jane clapped her hand over Annie's mouth.

"What is wrong with you two?" Jane asked. "If it wasn't for me, you'd have all of Dedman Street awake by now."

Annie pulled Jane's hand from her mouth. "What is that thing?" Annie asked.

Jane rolled her eyes. "Haven't you ever heard of a statue before?" she asked, shining her flashlight on the creature. The statue was nearly as tall as the room, and it looked like it was dressed for war. In one hand it held a sword; in the other it held Ben's shirt. "Your shirt just got stuck on this statue," Jane said as she reached over

43

and unhooked Ben's shirt from the statue's stiff fingers.

"This statue wasn't here before," Annie said. "It must be new."

"Then so is that," Ben said, pointing his flashlight to the far corner of the living room. His beam caught the frozen face of a hairy creature, part man and part beast. It stood in the corner right behind the couch.

"Where did the Hauntlys get these ugly things?" Annie said.

Jane shrugged. "I guess some people would call it fine art," she said. "They probably found them in an art museum."

"Either that," Ben said, "or a haunted house!"

"It doesn't matter," Annie said. "We don't have time to gawk at statues. We need to see what's in Hilda's laboratory."

The kids made their way down the dark hallway toward Hilda's laboratory. Cobwebs clung to their hair, and Annie was sure she heard mice darting around her feet. When they finally reached the door

Jane grabbed the doorknob. The door squeaked when she pulled it open.

Beakers and tubes filled with gurgling green liquids lined the shelves in the laboratory. Smoke rolled off the top of a big kettle. But that's not what got the kids' attention. All three of them shined the tiny beams of their flashlights on the tables in the center of the room.

The tables were completely empty.

Jane gasped. "This can only mean one thing," she said. "Whatever was on those tables is loose in Bailey City!"

Annie gulped. "The Hauntlys will be history if the mayor finds out they turned twin monsters loose on Dedman Street."

"We have to do something," Ben said. "Kilmer is our best friend."

"But what can we do?" Annie yelped.

"We have to find those monsters," Jane said. "Before it's too late."

"It's the only way we can save the Hauntlys," Ben said, "and Bailey City!"

"But it's dark out there," Annie whined. "Maybe we should wait until morning."

"Then it will be too late," Jane said. "We have to go now!"

Jane didn't wait for Annie to argue. She left Hilda's laboratory and made her way back down the hall. Ben and Annie followed close behind. Jane hurried toward the living room. She was almost there when the hallway flooded with lights.

"Oh, no!" Annie screamed. "We're caught!"

9
Midnight

Jane, Annie, and Ben slowly turned around. There stood Professor E. Gore. He grinned and licked his lips before speaking.

"What have we here?" Professor E. Gore asked.

Kilmer, Boris, and Hilda appeared at the top of the stairs just as a clock bonged twelve times.

"How lovely," Hilda said, "a party!"

Boris smiled so big, Annie could see his eyeteeth gleaming. "The stroke of midnight is my favorite time for a party," he said. "I'll just whip up a snack . . . with something nice and warm to drink."

Boris moved so fast, it looked like he glided down the stairs. Hilda and Kilmer followed behind him.

Professor E. Gore held out his hand,

stopping Boris from flying into the kitchen. "These children," he said, "they are perfect."

Ben stood up tall and grinned. "I know that," he said. "But my teachers just won't believe me."

Jane elbowed Ben. "I have a feeling that's not what he meant."

Professor E. Gore ignored Ben and spoke to Hilda. "They are smaller than the others," he told her. "The other . . . guests were much too large. That is why our project was a failure. We must start with something smaller. Like these children." With that, Professor E. Gore pointed a dirty fingernail at Annie, Jane, and Ben.

Jane gulped. "We would love to stay for the party," Jane finally said. "But it is way past our bedtime."

Annie nodded so hard she got dizzy. "We have to go home or we'll get in trouble."

"Double trouble," Ben said as Jane grabbed his arm and pulled him toward the front door.

Boris frowned. "But the party was just getting fun," he said. "Perhaps you will come back another night."

Annie didn't have a chance to answer because Jane pulled her out the front door. Then Jane slammed the wooden door and they all hurried down the steps and huddled under the dead branches of a tree in the Hauntlys' front yard.

"That was a close call," Annie said with a whoosh of air.

"This is worse than I ever imagined," Jane told her friends. "Professor E. Gore wants us for his experiments!"

"But that can only mean one thing," Annie said. "Professor E. Gore is planning to make doubles — of us!"

10

Kilmer to the Rescue

Clomp! Clomp! Clomp! Ben opened his eyes and stared at the blue sky. It was the day after they'd sneaked into Kilmer's house. He was in the tree house, lying on his back with his shoes and socks scattered on the tree house floor. Ben, Annie, and Jane had met back at the tree house as soon as the sun rose. They had to figure out how to save Bailey City from the evil Professor E. Gore. So far, they hadn't thought of a thing and Ben was getting tired of listening to the girls.

Clomp! Clomp! Clomp! It sounded like the end of the world.

Ben smiled and turned to see his friend Kilmer pop his head into the tree house. "Want to play soccer?" Kilmer asked.

"Sure," Ben said, hopping up. "That's the best idea I've heard all morning."

Jane grabbed Ben's arm. "You're not going anywhere, mister," Jane said. "You have to help us figure out what to do next."

"What's wrong?" Kilmer asked.

Ben started to talk, but Annie shook her head. "Maybe you shouldn't tell Kilmer."

Ben rolled his eyes. "Kilmer is our friend. We can tell him anything." Ben turned to Kilmer and told him, "Annie and Jane think someone is trying to steal Professor E. Gore's secrets."

Kilmer gasped. "Whatever gave you that horrible idea?"

"Because," Jane told Kilmer, "we saw a spy in the bushes outside Hilda's laboratory."

"Oh, no," Kilmer gasped. "This is terrible. We must find out who the spy is before he returns!"

"What makes you think the spy is coming back?" Annie asked.

"Because," Kilmer told his friends, "the

professor and my mother have not figured out the solution to their project. Whoever was listening will have to come back to discover how to complete the professor's process."

"Can't we just play soccer and forget all about it?" Ben asked.

"Professor E. Gore is a good family friend," Kilmer said. "I have to help him."

Annie nodded. "I'm glad someone around here is willing to help."

Ben fell back down on the tree house floor. He waved a white sock around like a flag. "All right, I give up. I'll help you."

"Do you have a plan?" Kilmer asked.

Jane shook her head. "We've been thinking all morning and we still don't know what to do."

"All we know is that someone was spying on Professor E. Gore from those bushes," Annie explained, pointing to the bushes outside the laboratory. "Ben tried to catch him by playing ape man, but it didn't work."

Jane giggled. "Ben ended up being a monkey in the garbage."

Ben stuck out his tongue at Jane and pulled out his rope. "I can't help it if my rope was too short."

Kilmer looked at Ben's rope and smiled. "I have an idea," Kilmer explained. "First, we have to watch for the spy. That will be my job. Someone else must watch for my signal when the spy returns."

"I can do that," Annie said.

Kilmer nodded. "I need someone to push off the secret weapon."

"I want to do that," Ben said.

"What can I do?" Jane asked.

Kilmer smiled. "I'm glad you asked. Because you get the hardest job of all."

11

Chicken

"No way!" Jane said after Kilmer told her what to do.

"Jane's a chicken! Jane's a chicken!" Ben teased.

Jane folded her arms and looked up from her perch on the tree house floor. "I'm not a chicken. I'm just smart enough to know when something is a bad idea. And Kilmer's plan is definitely a bad idea."

Annie put her hand on Jane's shoulder. "Kilmer's plan is the only one we have. Maybe we should give it a try."

"You're the one who said we need to save the world from Professor E. Gore's secret. Now here's your chance," Ben told Jane.

Jane rubbed her chin and looked at her

friends. "I guess you're right, but I still think this plan is a bad idea."

Kilmer clomped down the ladder. "It's settled. We'll catch the spy tonight."

"But first," Ben said, following Kilmer out of the tree house, "it's time for a little soccer action."

Jane and Annie joined Ben and Kilmer in a friendly game of soccer in Ben's backyard. Jane kicked the ball hard, but Kilmer's big feet gave Kilmer an extra advantage. He knocked the ball so hard it landed on Hauntly Manor Inn's front porch. Kilmer's cat, Sparky, yowled when the ball smashed her tail.

Sparky and another cat zoomed off the porch and raced toward the back of Hauntly Manor Inn. Annie brought the ball to her backyard before asking Kilmer, "When did you get another cat?"

Kilmer shook his head. "We only have Sparky."

"But I just saw another cat in your yard," Annie told Kilmer.

"Maybe that cat belongs to Professor E. Gore," Ben suggested.

Jane whispered under her breath, "Maybe that cat was *made* by Professor E. Gore."

Ben started to answer Jane, but he was interrupted by Professor E. Gore yelling to them from the Hauntly Manor porch. "Kilmer," Professor E. Gore called. "Please invite your friends over tomorrow. I need them for my project." Professor E. Gore's wild hair waved in the breeze and he still wore his stained lab coat.

Kilmer waved back to Professor E. Gore. "I'll bring them," Kilmer said.

Annie gulped and frowned at Ben. Jane pulled Annie away from Kilmer and whispered, "I hope this plan works tonight or we'll be in big trouble tomorrow."

"Professor E. Gore has given me an even better idea," Kilmer said. "I'll be right back." Kilmer disappeared inside Hauntly Manor Inn.

Twenty minutes later the kids were hard at work, sitting cross-legged on the tree house floor carefully filling balloons with different colors of paint. "Where did you get all this paint?" Ben asked Kilmer.

"Professor E. Gore has lots of it," Kilmer explained.

"Maybe after tonight we can use some of this paint to decorate our tree house," Jane suggested.

"And I bet Mom will let us have some old curtains, too," Annie said.

Ben held up a paint-covered hand. "Hold on just a minute. There's no way we're going to turn this tree house into a frilly girls' club," Ben said.

"Well, maybe we don't need curtains," Jane agreed, "but we could paint it with some neat designs."

Kilmer held up a balloon filled with paint. "I know how to paint a skull and crossbones," Kilmer said. "My cousin taught me."

"Cool," Ben said, loading a paint-filled balloon into a plastic grocery bag.

Annie and Jane looked at each other and sighed. A skull and crossbones were not the kind of decorations they had in mind for the tree house. "We have to concentrate on catching the spy now," Jane said.

"We will," Kilmer said. "This paint will mark the spy even if he manages to get away."

"What do you mean 'he'?" Jane asked. "The spy could be a girl."

"No way," Ben snapped. "All the famous spies are boys. Look at James Bond."

"Look at Mata Hari," Annie said.

"Who?" Jane, Ben, and Kilmer asked together.

"Mata Hari was a famous spy during World War One and she was a woman," Annie said. "I read about it in a magazine at school."

Ben scratched his cheek and got blue paint all over his face. "It doesn't matter who the spy is as long as we catch him — or her. And that's exactly what we're going to do tonight."

12

Street of the Dead

Ben, Annie, and Jane met in the tree house after dark. They were all dressed in black like spies. Ben even had his walkie-talkie strapped to his belt.

"Come in, tree house," the walkie-talkie screeched. It was Kilmer on the other walkie-talkie in Hauntly Manor Inn.

"Turn that down," Jane whispered. "Do you want everyone to know we're up here?"

Ben turned the volume on low and whispered into the walkie-talkie. "This is the tree house. We're in position. Over."

The kids sat for a long time, staring at Hauntly Manor Inn. Not a light shone anywhere in the huge inn. In fact, there were no lights shining in any windows in any of the houses on Dedman Street. "This looks like the street of the dead," Annie whispered nervously.

"Not anymore," Ben whispered. "Look." Sure enough, a light switched on inside the laboratory and at the same time the bushes rustled outside. The front porch light of Hauntly Manor Inn clicked on and off.

"That's Kilmer's signal," Annie said. "It's time."

"I still don't think this is such a good idea," Jane said. "What if Kilmer's parents get mad at us for getting paint in their bushes?"

Annie handed Jane the rope. "They won't care as long as we help Professor E. Gore," Annie told Jane. "Besides, we made the rope longer. It'll be fine."

Ben handed Jane the plastic bag filled with paint balloons. "All right," Ben said with a smile. "Go get them, Mata Hari."

Jane stuck out her tongue at Ben, grabbed the paint bag, closed her eyes, and clutched the rope. Ben and Annie gave Jane

a big push. *Swoosh!* Jane flew out over the Hauntlys' yard and straight toward the laboratory window. In an instant Jane released the paint balloons and swung back toward the tree house. Paint flew everywhere and the bushes exploded with sound.

Kilmer threw on the porch light and the kids ran to see who they'd caught. Loud cat screeching met them at the bushes. Ben flicked his flashlight on just in time to see Sparky and his fellow cat stick up all the hair on their backs and hiss.

Sparky and the other cat were covered with red, blue, and pink paint. The cats shook and paint splattered all over Kilmer, Annie, Jane, and Ben.

Ben laughed. "There are your spies. Good work, Mata Hari."

Jane groaned and wiped paint off her nose.

The next morning the four kids had to wash two very angry cats. By the time they were through, Jane, Ben, and Annie had scratches all over their arms. The two cats didn't scratch Kilmer.

"I still say there was a spy," Jane said as they tried to dry Sparky with a black towel.

Annie's eyes got big. "That means Professor E. Gore's secret isn't safe! The spy could still come back."

Kilmer shook his head. "No need to worry. Without his paint, the professor can do no more work. He will be leaving today."

Annie took the hose and sprayed down the bushes before asking Kilmer a question. "You never did tell us. Why did Professor E. Gore have all those paints?"

Kilmer wiped soapsuds off his large forehead. "Professor E. Gore is more than a scientist. He is also an artist. He has all kinds of art supplies."

"An artist?" Ben yelled, picking up a bucket of sudsy water. "Does he happen to make statues?"

Kilmer nodded. "Sure, he even gave us two of his latest creations."

Annie and Ben looked at each other and

nodded. "You're in double trouble," Ben told Jane. Then Ben chased Jane around the yard with the bucket of sudsy water. Annie sprayed Jane with the hose.

"Living here is so exciting!" Kilmer laughed. "You never know what will happen next on Dedman Street."

About the Authors

Marcia Thornton Jones and Debbie Dadey like to write about monsters. Their first series with Scholastic, **The Adventures of the Bailey School Kids,** has many characters who are *monsterously* funny. Now with the Hauntly family, Marcia and Debbie are in monster heaven!

Marcia and Debbie both used to live in Lexington, Kentucky. They were teachers at the same elementary school. When Debbie moved to Aurora, Illinois, she and Marcia had to change how they worked together. These authors now create monster books long-distance. They play hot potato with their stories, passing them back and forth by computer.

About the Illustrator

John Steven Gurney is the illustrator of both **The Bailey City Monsters** and **The Adventures of the Bailey School Kids.** He uses real people in his own neighborhood as models when he draws the characters in Bailey City. John has illustrated many books for young readers. He lives in Vermont with his wife and two children.